Tessa heard the sound _____ ler coins already in the M_____ of coins falling had an c_____ t a little electric thrill pass _____ led down into the centre of the tree, and peered through the cupped branches at Mr Martello.

'It's a new plan,' she said airily. 'I'm staying up in the tree for twenty-four hours. People can sponsor me or give a donation.'

The words came out as naturally and carelessly as if she had been planning them for hours . . .

A Fortune Branches Out is the third title in a riveting quartet of novels about a group of cousins living in a small New Zealand town.

Margaret Mahy is internationally recognized as one of today's best writers for young readers, her books having been translated into all the major languages of the world. Twice winner of the prestigious Carnegie Medal, she has also won the Esther Glen Award five times and the Observer Teenage Fiction Award once. Born in a country town in New Zealand, the oldest of a family of five with over twenty cousins in the surrounding neighbourhood, Margaret Mahy grew up with a strong sense of being part of a close family. She lives near Christchurch in New Zealand.

The *Cousins Quartet*
by
Margaret Mahy

published by Doubleday/Yearling:

THE GOOD FORTUNES GANG
A FORTUNATE NAME
A FORTUNE BRANCHES OUT
TANGLED FORTUNES

MARGARET MAHY

A FORTUNE BRANCHES OUT

Illustrated by John Farman

YEARLING BOOKS

A FORTUNE BRANCHES OUT
A YEARLING BOOK 0 440 86288 4

First published in Great Britain by Doubleday,
a division of Transworld Publishers Ltd

PRINTING HISTORY
Doubleday edition published 1993
Yearling edition published 1995

Set in Bembo by Falcon Graphic Art Ltd, Wallington, Surrey

Yearling Books are published by Transworld Publishers Ltd,
61–63 Uxbridge Road, Ealing, London W5 5SA,
in Australia by Transworld Publishers (Australia) Pty. Ltd,
15–25 Helles Avenue, Moorebank, NSW 2170,
and in New Zealand by Transworld Publishers (N.Z.) Ltd,
3 William Pickering Drive, Albany, Auckland.

Reproduced, printed and bound in Great Britain by
Cox & Wyman Ltd, Reading, Berks.

To Yvonne, Ron, Ken, Joan,
Joyce and Arthur –
my cousins from next door

CHAPTER ONE

Tessa could never understand why people were so critical of her wish to become a rich corporate executive with a cellular phone. Nobody ever criticized Dick Whittington for setting out to seek his fortune. She was sure Dick Whittington would have enjoyed having a cellular phone as well as a cat.

'Tessa, don't expect to be paid for every single thing you do around the house,' her mother, Marama, often said. 'Money isn't everything, you know.'

But if money wasn't everything, why did the world act as if it was? People *needed* it every day of their lives. 'Money doesn't buy happiness,' Marama had said, shaking her head at Tessa.

'Yes, it does,' Tessa cried, amazed that her mother couldn't see this for herself.

Television ads for lotteries and banks showed people being showered with money and looking radiantly happy. That was all Tessa wanted in life . . . to be radiantly happy and to have a cellular phone slung on her belt, just as the cowboy heroes in films about the Wild West carried their six-shooters. When she thought of her own savings nestling in the bank, Tessa felt something very *like* happiness. And, after all, she had *worked* to save it. She had washed cars, cleaned windows, cut lawns and weeded gardens. Saving that money had been like an adventurous game in which she had pitted her wits against the world, and come out on top. So why shouldn't she enjoy the feeling?

'Other girls love horses and ballet,' cried her mother despairingly. 'Why don't you?'

Tessa shrugged and wrinkled her forehead. Loving horses and ballet showed girls were warm-hearted and artistic, and if anybody loved making money, it meant that they were somehow • horrible.

'Horses and ballet *cost* a lot,' muttered Tessa, standing under the tree at the Bright Street corner and looking proudly at the stall she had set up there. 'Someone *pays* for them with money.'

'Talking to yourself?' asked her cousin, Pete Fortune, from behind his armful of cardboard cartons. As Tessa turned to answer, a sound like a wolf howling swept towards her, then past her and, finally, away from her.

'Yaaaaah! Fortune!' It was Grant Chilling, an old enemy, swinging dangerously around the Bright Street corner on his ten-speed bicycle.

'Dead-loss Chilling,' Pete said. 'What a drongo! OK! Let's get organized. First, we'll get the counter straight, and then we'll be in business, mate.' Every now and then he talked in rhyme, though he never wrote poetry.

Tessa took out a thin book with a neatly folded slip of paper sticking out of it. The book was called *Succeed and Grow Rich* by Ellington Fillmore. Ellington Fillmore's photograph smiled from the back cover. *You too can climb the ladder of success,* he was saying in bold red print. The book was full of his wise sayings, and the back cover was filled with compliments from executive vice-presidents, all of whom owed their success to Ellington Fillmore's good advice. Tessa believed that if she followed Ellington's good advice she, too, might become an executive vice-president, with a high-rise office, a computer, a fax machine and a laser printer. She might even become a president, telling mere vice-presidents how to do things. Tessa longed to succeed and grow rich.

This afternoon she was going to practise making money, but nobody could call her greedy because the money she made would all be for other people. Tessa and her cousins, the members of the Good Fortunes Gang, were setting up a white-elephant stall to raise money for the

National Telethon's appeal on behalf of senior citizens.

Having put the cartons down on the counter under the Bright Street tree, Pete looked around curiously. 'Where are the others?' he asked.

'Lorelei had to go home first and collect her white-elephant cakes,' Tessa said. 'Tracey and Jackson said they'd come later. But they're not bringing anything. Tracey said her family eats every single thing in the house. There's never anything left over.'

As a big truck lumbered down Main Road, a rush of diesel-smelling dust beat on Tessa's face and rustled the leaves over her head. She looked up into the tree. Sunshine dappled her face with warm patches. Tessa smiled. Her white-elephant stall would look sunny and inviting to anyone still coming out of the Hamburgerama on the opposite corner. It would lure them closer. As she watched, a car drove by with a big sticker in its back window. *Support New Zealand*, it said. *Support Telethon*.

That's just what I'm doing, Tessa thought proudly.

The National Telethon took place every three years, always on behalf of some good cause or other. For twenty-four hours one particular television channel had no sport, no news, no cartoons, no advertisements, no mini-series, no quiz shows. Celebrities from overseas, rock singers, and stars of British or Australian soap operas, worked for a night and a day in front of the cameras, joking, singing, laughing and reading out messages, challenges and promises of money phoned in by people. Large, important groups like Air New Zealand, or small private family groups could take their contributions, big or little, to television studios. And while they stood there, handing over their money, cameras and lights would focus on them, and the soap-opera stars would thank them and praise them for their kind hearts. Anyone could suddenly be a star. Telethon was like a great money party, sprawling across the whole country.

This year Tessa had decided to branch out on her own. *Organize people to organize themselves*, Ellington Fillmore advised. Tessa had organized the whole Fortune family . . . not only her cousins, but her uncles, aunts and grandparents, as well to bake biscuits and donate pots of last year's jam. Her goal was to sell a hundred things at a dollar each. She imagined herself arriving at the Telethon centre, specially set up in the Fairfield Town Hall, and saying carelessly, 'Here you are! A hundred dollars from the Fortune cousins.' Then she would give a small speech about being kind to senior citizens. She had it written out and hidden it in the back of *Succeed and Grow Rich*.

'Yaaaah! Fortune Finks!' howled Grant, cycling past again, but Tessa scarcely noticed him. She was too interested in arranging her white-elephant wares . . . an old lamp, a lumpy china vase with handles like ears, a candlestick shaped like a banana, and several bottles of her grandmother's famous plum jam. Tessa had also brought along an old adding machine she had found while spring-cleaning an office for her grandfather, but this was for adding up her profits. Her father had refused to lend her his calculator, even though it was only for the day. He said he needed it himself.

A shaggy-haired old man called Mr Martello stopped and stared at Tessa and Pete as they worked on the stall.

'I hope you tidy all that away afterwards,

Tessa,' he said severely. (All grown-ups ever worry about, thought Tessa, is tidying up afterwards.) 'It's a nice corner here,' Mr Martello went on. 'We don't want children playing shop and then leaving a lot of junk behind.'

Playing shop! Tessa was insulted.

'It's a white-elephant stall,' she said. 'We're raising money for the Telethon.'

'Telethon! Telethon!' cried Mr Martello in tones of despair. 'Where can I get away from it? Trampolin-athons! Rock-and-roll-athons! Are you part of the school sport-athon, then?'

'We're freelance,' explained Tessa. 'We're going to make a hundred dollars.' (Just saying it made her feel as if she had made that magical amount of money already.) 'It's for a good cause,' she added, because that was what they were saying at school and on television, too. *Support the Telethon. It's for such a good cause.* 'It's to help senior citizens.' *Like you,* she nearly added.

'Hmmmph!' said Mr Martello. 'All people talk about these days is money! I'm going to have my hair cut.'

He turned in the direction of the Top Storey Hair Salon. Tessa knew he was going to get *his* hair cut free, because his daughter-in-law worked at the salon. He would wait there, reading articles about Princess Di and Elizabeth Taylor in the hair-salon magazines, and his daughter-in-law would clip him in between the rinses and hairsets of paying customers. It is easy to speak scornfully of money when you are on the way to get a free haircut, thought Tessa.

Mr Martello stopped and looked back at her. It was as if he had suddenly tuned into her thinking.

'Money isn't everything, you know,' he said sternly.

'Yaaaah! Fortune!' shouted Grant Chilling, shooting past the tree once more. Ellington

Fillmore had no good advice about what vice-presidents should do if people like Grant Chilling rode past their offices shouting 'Yaaaaaah!' at them. *Have faith in yourself. Believe you are a winner and you will win*, he promised. I *will* have faith in myself, Tessa promised fervently. She wanted to be a winner more than anything else in the world. All the same, that mocking cry danced in her ears like a trapped echo long after Grant had vanished round the corner.

CHAPTER TWO

Bright Street, the street Tessa lived in, ended in a small, green lawn cut in half by the footpath. The council had put a garden seat there so that people could sit and watch the traffic go by, or stare at the tree . . . a shaggy-barked gum which looked like an umbrella turned inside out. When the tree was much younger, the council had cut out its centre so that it would not grow too tall. Now, its branches curved like grasping fingers, springing from around a wide, blunt scar. It was under this tree that Tessa and Pete had erected the stall.

Directly opposite stood Sampson's Hamburgerama and Fish and Chips Shop. To the left, on the other side of Bright Street, was a pet shop called Fish 'n' Cheeps. Next to Fish 'n'

Cheeps was a small general store, Chillings Superette, which sold milk and ice creams, pet food, and frozen peas and string — indeed, everything anyone might need suddenly during the weekend when all the other shops were closed.

Pete and Tessa spread their white-elephant goods across the counter they had made from apple-boxes, planks and a small stepladder . . . home-made biscuits, summer seedlings in old yoghurt cartons, paperback detective stories with peeling spines, baby clothes donated by Tessa's older sister, Prue. On top of one carton sat a big monkey made of plastic, which was a money box as well as being a toy. There was a slit in the top

WHITE ELEPHANT TELETHON STALL

of the monkey's hat to drop your money through. When you needed to count it, you simply unscrewed the monkey's head. Tessa would have preferred a real cash box with a lock, but the Money Monkey would have to do.

Pete began arranging the bags of biscuits which he said he had made the night before. Tessa, however, knew his mother must have helped him.

While Pete lovingly set his biscuits out in a straight line along the front of the counter, Tessa began to tack up the sign she had made on Wednesday night.

GOOD FORTUNES GANG WHITE-ELEPHANT TELETHON STALL, it said. She thought TESSA'S TELETHON STALL would have sounded a lot neater, but, after all, she and her cousins were in this together.

A woman walked by, pausing to read the poster.

'You kind children,' she said. 'It's such a good cause, isn't it? We owe a lot to senior citizens.'

Then she bought a bag of biscuits.

'See? We've made money already!' cried Tessa as soon as the woman had gone. 'And we haven't really begun yet.'

She dropped fifty cents through the slot in the top of the Money Monkey's hat. It echoed as it fell. Tessa tapped in the figure '50' into the old adding machine and pulled the handle down. The paper roll jiggled and inched forward.

'You said we'd sell things for a dollar each,' hissed Pete. 'We'll never get a hundred dollars.'

'This is just a beginning,' Tessa said. 'And I haven't even put up the picture yet. We're not official until the picture's up.'

The picture Tessa had painted last night was one of the best she had ever done. It showed two rosy senior citizens waving small bagfuls of money, and kicking up their heels with happiness. In between them danced a big white elephant, playing music out of its trunk. Above the

elephant's head floated a billowing cloud which
was also a speech balloon. 'Now you will be able
to afford singing lessons *and* your knee operation,'
the elephant was saying in bright pink lettering.
'Thanks to TELETHON you will be able to sing
and dance for ever and a day.' Pete looked over
Tessa's shoulder as she pinned up the picture.

'That elephant looks drunk,' he said. 'People
might think that senior citizens will be spending
the Telethon money on whisky.'

'It's happy,' Tessa said indignantly. 'They're
having a great time.' She loved her own picture. It
had flowed out of her pens and paintbrushes as if
it had been secretly waiting for the chance to get
out on to paper. It wasn't often that a picture
seemed to paint itself like that.

Grant Chilling shot by on his bike once more.
'Ha ha ha–HA ha!' he cried, like a motor horn.
This time Tessa felt really irritated with him. It
wasn't fair. It just wasn't fair.

'Shut *up*!' she yelled, but he was already round
the corner and heading down Main Road, flitting
off for the moment like a mosquito, but already
planning to buzz and sting again.

And it was only a few minutes before he came
by once more bringing his only friend, Conrad
Eddy, to buzz and sting with him.

Chilling and Eddy, thought Tessa. This means
trouble. She sighed. But Ellington Fillmore
smiled from the back of the book cover. *In order to
win, you must really want to be a winner*, he said.

And Tessa did want to be a winner. She felt she
wanted it more than anything else in the world.

CHAPTER THREE

A woman came out of the Top Storey Hair Salon, and turned towards the stall under the tree. She wore high heels and carried a patchwork bag over one shoulder.

'A customer,' hissed Pete.

'A client!' Tessa corrected him quickly. People in supermarkets were customers. 'Client' sounded much more professional.

'Finky Fortune!' yelled Grant, but Tessa was too busy being professional to take any notice.

'Your hair looks great,' she said admiringly as the woman went by. (Ellington Fillmore said you should find something nice to say to clients.)

'Nice try, kid!' said the woman, and laughed. But she stopped all the same, running her eye over the biscuits, the shrunken baby clothes and the vase.

'Oh dear,' said the woman. 'I've got enough junk of my own already.' But then she saw the candlestick shaped like a banana and began to laugh. 'I'll take this,' she said. 'It's my sister's birthday next week. We always give one another crazy presents.'

'A dollar,' said Pete, pretending to look at the price.

'You must be joking!' said the woman. 'It's expensive at fifty cents. I reckon I'm doing you a favour taking it off your hands, mate.' She slapped a coin down on the counter. 'Don't bother to wrap it.'

Tessa sighed as the banana-shaped candlestick vanished into the patchwork bag and was carried off past Fish 'n' Cheeps.

'If we only get fifty cents for everything,' she said, 'we'll have to sell two hundred things. I don't think we've got that much stuff . . . I mean that much product.'

Calling pots of plum jam and shrunken baby clothes *product* made her feel professional all over again.

Mrs Meadowes, from the house next to Tessa's, came down Main Road and turned into Bright Street. She stopped, too, and bought a yoghurt carton of cornflower plants.

'I hope they're blue,' she said. 'Cornflowers ought to be blue. I'm not crazy about pink ones. And are those biscuits hard?'

She poked at one biscuit through the plastic bag and it crumbled a little.

'No,' replied Tessa. 'They're crisp.'

'Oh, they're crisp!' cried a silly, squeaky voice. It was Grant, standing with Conrad, one telegraph pole down Bright Street. Mrs Meadowes pulled a face.

'My word,' she said, 'if I was that one's

mother, I'd have something to say to him.' She took the biscuits and cornflowers, paid two dollars, and went in through her gate, slamming it behind her.

'They're crisp! They're crisp!' yelled Grant. He and Conrad leaped on to their bikes again and began biking round and round the stall, swerving in closer and closer. They had really begun to annoy Tessa.

'Fortune cookies!' screamed Conrad. 'Hey, Tessa, are you a Fortune cookie?'

'Get out!' she yelled, and turned to Pete. 'Here comes another client. Get rid of Grant!'

'Me?' said Pete dubiously. But he ran at Grant and Conrad, who simply swerved away, laughing and jeering. Tessa could see that Pete had no chance of catching them.

CHAPTER FOUR

While two more clients were eyeing an ancient lamp, a shiny red Escort drew up beside the stall. Tessa recognized the car at once. In it were her aunt, Lorna Bancroft, and her cousin, Lorelei. Lorelei's father, Ivor, was the only person Tessa actually knew who had a cellular phone, but then he was the manager of the bank and responsible for Tessa's own savings.

Lorelei scrambled out of the Escort and ran round to the back to open the boot. She lifted out a box and, carrying it very carefully, brought it over to the stall. Inside, was a beautiful cake, iced with soft, pale chocolate icing, piped with darker chocolate around the edges, and set with crystallized cherries and angelica.

'Gosh, it seems wrong to eat this cake,' Tessa said, thinking it was beautiful enough to wear. The cake made everything else on the white-elephant stall look shabby and old.

'Oh dear!' said one of the clients. 'Just when I'm on a diet. Is this cake only a dollar?'

'Two dollars,' said Pete quickly. Lolly, who was running back to the car, turned and made a face at them. Then she picked up another box, identical to the first.

'I'll take it,' said the woman. 'You'd pay ten dollars for a cake like this at the Cream Castle,' she added to her friend.

Cream Castle was the smartest bakery in Fairfield.

Lorelei set off to the car for the third time. She had brought three cakes with her, all equally beautiful.

'I'll collect you round about six o'clock,' Aunt Lorna was shouting to Lorelei, waving and smiling from the driver's seat. The red Escort slid off, sounding as glossy as it looked.

'Did Auntie Lorna make these?' asked Pete, gazing greedily at the cakes.

'No way!' said Lolly, waving as her mother vanished round the corner. 'She makes good casseroles, but she's hopeless with cakes. She bought them for us from Cream Castle. They're her donation to Telethon.'

Tessa was shocked. She had sold a ten–dollar cake for two dollars. Not only that — the clients, after a brief discussion on the other side of Bright Street, were coming back across the road.

'I'll buy one, too,' said the cakeless client, slapping two dollars down on the white tablecloth. Tessa was about to charge this client five dollars, when she caught the woman's beady stare and found she didn't quite have the courage to tell her that the price had suddenly gone up.

Conrad and Grant came biking past yet again. The sight of a customer paying money over the white tablecloth seemed to infuriate them.

'I wouldn't pay ten cents for your rotten stuff,' Grant yelled. He saw a man coming down the Main Road footpath past Top Storey. 'Don't buy anything from them,' he yelled. 'Their dog peed on the cakes.'

The man looked startled and kept to the far edge of the footpath, turning his head away from the white-elephant stall. Tessa tried to reassure him.

'I haven't even *got* a dog,' she called as he went by.

'Fresh biscuits and cakes,' cried Pete invitingly, but the man stared fixedly across Main Road at the Hamburgerama.

'Yaaaaah!' yelled Grant and Conrad triumphantly.

'He wouldn't have bought anything, anyway,' said Lorelei. 'He had a non-buying face.'

'Hey!' exclaimed Pete suddenly. He had picked up the styrofoam tray that held cartons of cornflower plants, and was staring into the box underneath it. 'What did you bring these old tins for? They're empty.'

There were fifteen small tins, and on each one there was a picture of a woman with a sunhat and an armful of yellow leaves. *Golden Haze Tobacco*, proclaimed the words on the top of each tin.

'I found them when I was cleaning out an old desk at the back of the empty shed at the grandys',' said Tessa. 'Those tins were Great-Grandy Fortune's secret.'

'The one with the geraniums on his grave,' said

Pete, who lived next to the old town cemetery and knew the names on the graves by heart.

'He was supposed to stop smoking,' Tessa explained, 'but he used to sneak into Grandpa Fortune's office and smoke there secretly. The bottom drawer of the desk had all these old tobacco tins hidden in it.'

'He lived to be ninety-seven. It's on his gravestone,' said Pete.

'If he hadn't smoked he'd have lived to be a hundred,' said Tessa. 'Or a hundred-and-ten!'

Conrad and Grant had propped their bikes against the Meadowes' hedge, and came walking towards the stall with mincing steps, pretending to be real clients.

'Oh look, a rubbish shop under the tree,' said Grant. 'You need rubber gloves and a gas mask to go shopping there. Stinky *old* stuff. Stink! Stink!' he yelled.

'Get out!' shrieked Tessa. 'This stuff is for proper clients.'

'I'm allowed to look at a stall on a public street!' said Grant. 'You can't stop me!' He rattled money in his pockets.

A man and a woman came out of Fish 'n' Cheeps. They had two small, white, fluffy dogs on red leads. The dogs ran with twinkling, rapid steps on paws that were almost invisible under their fluffy coats. It looked as if they were trundling along on wheels.

'I always go through second-hand books,' the man said to the woman as they approached the stall. 'I just might come across some treasure.'

'The vase is cheap,' said Lolly invitingly.

'It would need to be,' said the woman, and laughed sarcastically.

Grant and Conrad, knowing they were safe, came right up to the counter, elbowing each other and giggling. They even jostled the man as he looked at the books.

'Hey, stop that,' growled Pete.

'Yes! Stop that, Grant Chilling,' cried Lorelei and Tessa in a scolding duet.

'Make me!' said Grant, stepping on one of the little dogs. It began a piteous yelping. Both Pete and Tessa came round from behind the counter. The clients moved on hastily, taking their dogs with them, shooting angry glances over their shoulders. Conrad poked at one of the packets of biscuits. Tessa tried to push his hand away. The bag of biscuits fell to the ground.

'Ugh!' yelled Grant. 'Throw them out. They've been on the ground.'

'They're wrapped in plastic,' said Tessa, brushing dirt off the bag.

'It doesn't matter,' said Conrad. 'If you try and sell them to anybody, I'll tell them those biscuits have been lying on the ground.'

Then he made a scooping gesture over the last of the Cream Castle cakes. He did not quite touch it, but he certainly threatened it. Tessa suddenly felt as if she were standing quite bare in a cold, southerly wind, while being attacked by special cold-weather mosquitoes, flying in much faster than she could slap them away. The stall, the cake, the books and the biscuits suddenly felt like a living part of Tessa, a part which needed protection.

Tessa ran at Grant but he skipped away, and while she was chasing him, Conrad swept his arm across the counter, knocking the books all over the ground. Then Pete was on him, and they wrestled wildly until Conrad brought his knee up hard into Pete's stomach. Pete sat down heavily. His mouth sagged open. He had a stunned look and made a whooping sound, as if he were struggling to get air into his lungs.

'Ha! Ha!' shrieked Grant, dancing away from Tessa.

'I'm the karate king!' yelled Conrad, dancing too, though he looked a little surprised at his own success. He had to shout because two heavy trucks were going by, swallowing all other noises with their roar.

'Fortune cookies! Fortune cookies!' yelled Grant.

Then he somehow zoomed around Tessa, and snatched up the vase.

'Hey, look at this!' he said, tossing it to Conrad who caught it and threw it back. Lorelei dashed from behind the counter to help Pete stagger to his feet, looking as if he could not straighten up properly.

'Stop that!' Tessa cried, as the vase flew through the air again. 'That's an antique.'

'Make me stop it!' Grant called triumphantly.

As he spoke, he was grabbed from behind. It all took place so quickly that even Tessa did not quite see how it happened. She was as surprised as Grant, and he was horrified. He yelled and wriggled.

'She told you to *stop it*,' someone said in his ear.

It was Tracey Fortune – fierce Tracey – and her brother, Jackson. The trucks going past had swallowed the noise of the approaching skateboard wheels. Grant had danced right back into Tracey's arms, just as she had leaped off her skateboard, letting it run freely on to the grass. Now she threw her wiry arms around him and held him so tightly he could not get away. She squeezed him and then shook him from side to side, as if she were a terrier dealing with a rat.

CHAPTER FIVE

'Did you say, *make me stop*?' asked Tracey. She was a tanned, tall girl with white-blonde hair, and eyes so blue they were startling in her sunburned face. Jackson, her younger brother of nine, stood beside her wearing black sunglasses that were a little too big for him.

'Let him go!' yelled Conrad. Though he was just as tall as Tracey, Tessa could see that Tracey alarmed him. Quickly passing the vase back to Lorelei, he turned to watch Tracey dealing with Grant.

'Listen, Eddy,' Tracey said. 'If you come one step closer, Chilling will really suffer. I'll bite his ear off.'

Tracey's mouth looked dangerously close to Grant's ear.

'Keep away!' screamed Grant. Tessa was amazed at his sudden fear. Ellington Fillmore had no useful advice about what an executive should do if one of the workforce threatened to bite off a competitor's ear. Not only that: it was all too easy to imagine Mrs Chilling erupting out of Chillings Superette to protect her young.

'Don't hurt him, Trace!' Tessa cried anxiously.

'The last boy that said *make me stop* to a Fortune is a sad boy these days,' said Tracey ominously. 'He can't hear anything.'

'No ears, man, no ears!' sang Jackson, strumming an imaginary guitar.

The strange thing was that Grant, who had seemed so tough a few moments ago, now looked small and pathetic, writhing in Tracey's grip.

'Were you interested in my cousin's white elephants, Chilling?' asked Tracey. 'Help him, General Jackson.' She hooked one of her arms forcibly through Grant's. Jackson seized the other arm. Grant lurched a step forward. Tracey and Jackson hauled him back. He dragged behind and they tugged him forward. Between them, they hauled him over to the stall and stood him in front of the vase he had been so carelessly tossing around a moment earlier.

'Great vase!' cried Tracey enthusiastically. 'Isn't it great, Chilling? Hey, your mother would love this for a present, wouldn't she?'

Grant struggled to unhook his arm from Tracey's.

'I know you like that vase,' Tracey muttered into his ear.

Grant didn't say anything.

'Don't you?' she asked, nudging him.

'It's OK!' said Grant in a small, weak voice.

'OK? That's not good enough. Say, "I think that vase is the prettiest thing I've seen all day",' Tracey commanded him.

'I think that vase is very p–p–pretty,' stuttered Grant obediently. Tessa saw with horror that he was really frightened. Conrad watched from a distance, alarmed and fascinated, like an antelope watching another antelope being devoured by a lion.

'I reckon Grant would like to *buy* this vase for his mother,' said Tracey. 'Don't you think he'd like to buy it, Jackson?'

'Sure do,' said Jackson. 'You and that vase go together, man, except the vase is way out prettier.'

'Say, "I'd really like to buy that vase",' Tracey said to Grant. He was silent. 'Go on, say it!' she hissed in his ear.

'I'd like to b–b–buy . . .' Grant began. He was stammering again.

Tessa had forgotten that two years ago Grant had stammered almost all the time. It wasn't fair. In spite of all Grant's teasing and tormenting, she was beginning to feel sorry for him.

'Say it loudly,' commanded Tracey, 'so everyone can hear.'

Grant was silent as he swallowed, trying to get his words in order. It must be terrible, thought Tessa, to be as frightened as Grant was. How had everything become so serious so suddenly? She looked up and down the street. A woman was hauling a complaining dog with a pointed nose into Fish 'n' Cheeps, but there wasn't a possible client in sight.

'Make him promise to leave us alone,' Pete said to Tracey. He was breathing easily again. 'Then let him go.'

'Let him go?' Tracey cried indignantly. 'He'd just ride off laughing at us. Go on, Chilling. Say, "I'd like to buy this vase." '

'I'd like to b–b–buy this vase,' stammered Grant.

'Right! Now *buy* it!' said Tracey.

Grant put his hand into his pocket, as he glanced timidly into Jackson's dark glasses. He brought out three coins . . . a dollar, a fifty-cent piece and a five-cent piece.

'This vase is terribly cheap,' said Tracey. 'It's a dollar fifty.'

'No, it isn't,' said Tessa. 'It's only twenty cents.'

'You'll never make a hundred dollars,' said Tracey, but she didn't argue. She seemed rather puzzled by Grant . . . someone who gave in so easily; someone who suddenly seemed to have thin, hollow bones like a bird's. Tracey looked over at Conrad. 'Hey, what sort of friend are you, anyway?' she asked scornfully.

'You said you'd bite his ear off,' Conrad reminded her.

'Me? Bite his ear off?' Tracey cried. 'I wouldn't bite *his* ear. Ugh! Yuck! I brushed my teeth this morning. Now, listen! If either of you gives my cousins a hard time I'll *get* you sooner or later. Because Jackson and I hear everything and go everywhere, don't we, Jackson?'

'Sure do, man! Here, there and everywhere,' said Jackson. His sunglasses slipped sideways.

Tracey let Grant go. He ran for his bike.

'Hey, Chilling!' called Tracey. Grant stopped as if he were on a lead, and she had jerked him to a standstill. 'You forgot your vase!'

Grant came back and took the vase from the counter. Tessa saw that tears were running down his cheeks. It couldn't have been from pain. Tracey had not actually hurt him. It might have been from fear, but, after all, the worst was over. It occurred to Tessa that he might have been crying from a sort of shame. She looked over at Tracey who smiled at her.

'Thanks for stopping him,' Tessa said doubtfully.

Her thanks sounded faint and uncertain. Tracey's smile vanished.

'You *wanted* him to stop, didn't you?' asked Tracey.

'Yes,' said Tessa, 'but I didn't want you to . . . to hurt his *feelings*.'

Tracey stared at her.

'Oh, terrific!' she said after a moment. 'No hurt feelings! Right!'

Tessa felt that now, in some way she did not understand, she had actually hurt Tracey's feelings by not appreciating the protection Tracey had given her.

Tracey nudged Jackson.

'Come on, General,' she said. 'Let's split!'

'Right on!' Jackson said, straightening his sunglasses.

They set off together, going back up Main Road.

Tessa was about to shout some word of thanks after her vanishing cousins. But then she saw a group of clients . . . three women, two of them with pushchairs, coming down Main Road towards the tree.

Always see the positive side of new business opportunities, urged Ellington Fillmore.

'The show must go on,' Tessa said, pushing things together so that the counter looked crowded again. Pete was gathering the books from the ground. The cake, luckily, had hardly been touched.

'Support Telethon,' Tessa called as the women came towards her, and they stopped to browse and choose and smile, sliding a few coins into the Money Monkey.

CHAPTER SIX

About fifteen minutes later, Mrs Chilling came marching out of the Chillings Superette holding the vase in front of her by one of its china ears as if she could scarcely bear to touch it. She did not look at the stall under the tree, but crossed the road and vanished through Tessa's gateway.

'She looks mad, mad, mad,' muttered Pete. 'It's going to be bad, bad, bad.'

Shortly after that, Tessa heard her mother calling her. She turned round guiltily. Her mother and Mrs Chilling were marching down Bright Street, side by side.

'Tessa,' her mother said, sounding irritated and tired. 'Will you come here for a moment?'

'We'll watch the stall,' murmured Lorelei.

Mrs Chilling and Tessa's mother, Marama, met her halfway between the gate and the stall.

'Mrs Chilling says that one of you grabbed Grant and forced him to buy this vase,' Marama said crossly.

'I didn't,' said Tessa.

'Apparently it was one of Peter Fortune's kids,' said Mrs Chilling. 'The oldest one — that great, big, rough girl.'

In a way, it was a fair description of Tracey. But Tessa recalled Ellington Fillmore's instructions. *Support your sales force.*

'Tracey's only a little bit taller than Grant,' she cried. 'Anyhow, Grant and Conrad were jostling my clients. They knocked bags of biscuits on to the ground. And they grabbed that vase and threw it around.'

Marama looked accusingly at Mrs Chilling.

'A little bit of horseplay is quite different from deliberate bullying,' Mrs Chilling cried. 'Grant's a very sensitive boy, and now he's in a fearful state. His money was taken from him. You Fortune kids ganged up on him. It was five against one. Ask Conrad Eddy!'

'No!' cried Tessa. 'Truly, it wasn't.' She looked at her mother, but her mother's expression was grim. 'Grant and Conrad yelled at us, and called us names, and began to take our stuff, and Conrad hit Pete in the stomach and hurt him. No-one hurt Grant. Tracey just grabbed him because he was being such a pain.'

Mrs Chilling took no notice of her. She looked at Marama, instead.

'Five against one,' she said. 'All he wanted to do was to join in the fun. It wouldn't have hurt them to ask him to help, would it? And now he's at the back of the shop, sobbing his heart out.'

'It's not because he's hurt,' Tessa said. 'It's just that nobody likes him.'

But this was the wrong thing to say. Mrs Chilling looked furious.

'He's stammering again. It was nasty bullying,'

she said to Marama. 'I'm sorry. I want something done about it, or I'm getting in touch with someone — the school. Or the council!'

'Tessa,' said Marama. 'Pack up your stall. It's causing too much trouble.'

Tessa tried to recall every bit of good advice in Ellington Fillmore's book, but there was nothing to tell you what to do if your mother sided with the enemy and made you close down your business.

'But he knocked our biscuits on to the ground,' she wailed. 'And Conrad tried to stick his finger in our Cream Castle cake.'

Both women suddenly looked impressed. Cakes from Cream Castle were not to be fingered by Conrad Eddy. Then Mrs Chilling pulled herself together again.

'I can't be responsible for Conrad Eddy, too,' she said.

'Sorry, Tessa! At once!'

'Mum, it's for Telethon. It's for a good cause.'

'No,' said her mother. 'I know Tracey wouldn't hurt Grant, but she scared him badly. And he hasn't . . .' (she paused) '. . . he hasn't got anywhere else to play except around here.'

'I have to work,' said Mrs Chilling, as if Marama had accused her of deserting Grant. 'I'm

47

not like some people who can spend all day at home if they want to.'

'It's not fair!' Tessa cried, looking pleadingly at her mother.

'Maybe not,' said Marama, 'but the corner belongs to everyone, and neighbours are neighbours. I must say, Muriel,' she said to Mrs Chilling, 'it sounds as if Grant was being a real nuisance.'

'You Fortunes always stick together, right or wrong,' said Mrs Chilling. 'Not all of us have a townful of relatives to back us up. And I want the money you stole from him, too.'

Tessa went back to the stall. She gave Mrs Chilling twenty cents. Mrs Chilling returned the vase in stony silence, and marched back across the road.

'We have to stop,' Tessa told Lolly and Pete. 'We have to take everything inside again.'

Suddenly she knew she was going to cry. The workforce should never see a good manager burst into tears, even if they happen to be cousins as well as workers. Tilting her head back so that the tears could not run out of her eyes, Tessa pulled the poster and the picture of the dancing senior citizens away, but the tears somehow got into her nose. A sad wind blew down Main Road and

spun round the corner. The Telethon poster
rustled away down Bright Street, and the senior-
citizens poster, which was painted on cardboard,
went cartwheeling, end over end, off on its own.

Pete and Lorelei folded the tablecloth in silence, and then began packing up the planks. Tessa could feel their sympathy, but somehow it only made her disappointment worse. Salty tears started to drip out of her nose and ran back into her throat, while possible clients went by, glancing curiously at the dismantling of the stall.

Pete propped the ladder against the tree, and rattled the Money Monkey. 'Well, we've got something,' he said comfortingly.

Suddenly, Grant appeared at the door of Chillings Superette. He grabbed his bicycle, which was leaning beside the door, and cycled past them once more.

'Yaaahh!' he called triumphantly.

Tessa could not bear it. She wished that a cave would open at her feet. She would not hesitate to dive straight in, to live underground with worms and beetles for ever.

Instead, she ran up the ladder and into the tree, scrambling into the big cup of branches. Then she climbed up along one branch, higher and higher, until she could see more sky than ground. There she sat, pretending there was no Telethon and no town, imagining herself to be the only person in a rustling, leafy world. She did not even think about the wisdom of Ellington Fillmore any more. Nothing in his book, not even the words printed in capitals, could help a disappointed financial director forced to climb a tree to hide her tears.

CHAPTER SEVEN

It was like being in a green room with all sorts of misshapen windows. Looking directly ahead, Tessa found she could see straight down Main Road which was growing busier as the day wore on. By evening there would be lots and lots of people outside the Hamburgerama opposite. And people would be going to Chillings Superette because they suddenly needed milk or cat food. This would have been a great time to collect money for Telethon.

As she watched, a horse and cart came down the road. The cart was decorated with streamers, and the driver wore a wig and a mask.

Pony Clubs Collection for Telethon, read a splashy notice on the side of the cart. Girls in hard hats and jodhpurs were jumping off the cart and rattling boxes invitingly at passers-by. Those people giving money could have been *my* clients, thought Tessa bitterly.

Below, she heard footsteps in Bright Street. Pete had taken two of the cartons into Tessa's house. Now, he was coming back, and Marama was with him.

'Tessa!' she called from the foot of the tree. 'Come on down, dear. We'll be making a contribution from the firm, and you can take it in if you like.'

'*I* wanted to raise the money,' Tessa cried. 'I wanted us kids to do it ourselves.'

'I always feel so sorry for that wretched Grant,'

Marama explained. 'Tracey can be rough at times.'

'She just sort of stood over him, and talked at him,' said Pete. 'She didn't hurt him.'

At that moment, Grant went by on his bike again.

'Ha, ha ha-*ha* ha!' he called rudely, and then, suddenly seeing Tessa's mother, he put his head down and biked off fast.

'See?' cried Lorelei and Pete together.

'Oh dear,' said Tessa's mother. 'It's so hard to be *fair*. Come on down, Tessa. I'll make a little treat for dinner . . . a cake or something.'

'I want my *stall* not a *cake*!' Tessa cried. 'I've got a cake already — a cake from Cream Castle.'

'I can't beat that,' said Marama, laughing but sounding a little sad, too. 'Oh well . . .' She turned, and, looking down between leaves and twigs, Tessa watched her mother walk back down the road and in at her own gate once more.

'Well, what's going on here?' someone asked. It was Mr Martello, unusually spick and span, walking home with his hair and moustache freshly trimmed.

'Given up on the retail trade? What are you up to now? Oh well . . . better not ask. As long as it's a good cause.' Tessa heard the sound of a coin falling on top of other coins already in the Money Monkey.

The sound of coins falling had an odd effect on Tessa. She felt a little electric thrill pass through her. She scrambled down into the centre of the tree, and peered through the cupped branches at Mr Martello.

'It's a new plan,' she said airily. 'I'm staying up in the tree for twenty-four hours. People can sponsor me or give a donation.'

The words came out as naturally and carelessly as if she had been planning them for hours.

'You? Sit up all night in the tree?' exclaimed Mr Martello. 'I'll pay you a dollar for every hour you stay there. How about that?'

'Done!' cried Tessa.

'It's a bargain,' said Mr Martello. 'Get your lawyer to call mine.'

As he went down Bright Street, Tessa could hear him laughing to himself.

If your strategy is not working, be prepared to change it, Ellington Fillmore had said in chapter three of his book. Tessa had just changed her strategy.

'Fetch me some cardboard, a notebook and my felt pens,' Tessa commanded her workforce. 'I'm going to do a tree-athon poster. And we need a book for sponsors to write their names and addresses in.'

CHAPTER EIGHT

TREE-ATHON, said the new poster. TESSA FORTUNE IS STAYING IN THE TREE FOR TWENTY-FOUR HOURS. SPONSOR THE TREE-ATHON, OR MAKE A DONATION TO TELETHON.

Pete nailed the new poster to the shaggy trunk of the gum tree.

'I'm her manager,' he said to passers-by. 'I collect the money.' He rattled the Money Monkey to prove it.

One woman laughed and made a donation.

'How much?' Tessa called down.

'Only twenty cents,' said Pete. 'We're back to our pre-Chilling rate.'

'Pass me up the adding machine,' commanded Tessa.

There was a whirr of wheels far down the road. Two familiar figures came speeding towards the corner. Two skateboards stopped suddenly, spinning on their back wheels.

Pete and Lorelei both began talking at once, telling Tracey and Jackson what had been happening.

'. . . Mrs Chilling came over to see Auntie Marama . . .'

'. . . we had to give back the money you made Grant give us . . .'

Tracey pulled a fearsome face.

'Grant Chilling will meet his doom,' she said ominously.

'Forget him,' Tessa said. 'We've started a tree-athon. It's working out better.'

'Will people pay just to see you sit in a tree?' asked Jackson. 'I wouldn't.'

'He hasn't got any money, anyway!' Tracey said with a snort. 'But you could sing or do something. Don't just *sit* there.'

Tessa felt that faint electric thrill again.

'Pass me up one of the planks,' she said. 'I'll make a shelf for the adding machine.'

A man in a smart tweed jacket with leather patches on the elbows stopped to look at the remains of the white-elephant stall. He didn't look twice at the jam, or the Cream Castle cake, but the lamp interested him for a moment.

A couple of women strolled up, and Jackson called to them.

'See that girl in the tree?' he cried. 'She's going to sit up there all night to raise money for Telethon.'

The two women stared up at Tessa. The man put the lamp down, glanced at the vase, then looked away hastily.

'It's not safe,' said one of the women.

'We'll be guarding her,' said Tracey. 'Jackson and me. We're getting our pup tent and sleeping under the tree.'

'I am, too,' said Pete. 'Would you like to sponsor her at twenty cents an hour?'

'Well, you've got to admit that they're trying,' said the woman, grinning a little. She wrote her name and address in the sponsorship notebook. Twenty cents an hour.

'I'll bet Telethon never sees a cent of that money,' the cousins heard the other woman say as they walked away.

'Will Mum let us sleep out here all night?' Jackson asked Tracey.

'We'll ask in a *cunning* way,' Tracey said.

As her cousins argued at the foot of the tree, Tessa began setting up an office among the branches.

'A *branch* office,' she said, and smiled to herself.

Two old ladies came by, fresh from the Top Storey Hair Salon, their hair looking very white and fluffy and smelling strongly of hair lacquer. They, too, stopped to read the new poster nailed to the tree.

'What will they think of next?' exclaimed the taller of the two, looking up at Tessa and laughing.

'What?' yelled her companion.

'The little children are helping the Telethon, dear,' yelled the first woman, pointing at Tracey who was taller than she was.

'What?' yelled the second one, fiddling with her hearing aid.

61

'She's doing it for the Telethon, man,' yelled Jackson, rattling the Money Monkey rhythmically in her direction.

The first woman popped a dollar coin into the Money Monkey. The second one stared in astonishment at the Money Monkey being rattled in front of her. Then, opening her bag, she did the same. Other pedestrians stopped, too, wondering what was going on.

Tessa jammed boards between two branches to make shelves. She put the adding machine and the old desk calendar side by side, and suddenly she felt she really did have an office, even if it was up in a tree.

'Where did you get these?' asked the man in the tweed jacket suddenly. He had come across the carton of old tobacco tins.

'They were hidden in the bottom drawer of my grandfather's desk,' Pete said. 'My great-grandfather hid them there. The poor old joker was a secret smoker.'

No-one was listening to his rhyme so he had to laugh at it himself.

But Tracey and Jackson were impatient to be gone. They seized their skateboards. Off they went, sliding across Bright Street, going home to collect their pup tent.

'My own grandfather used to smoke this brand,' said the man, rattling one of the tobacco tins curiously. 'Suppose I give you . . . let me see . . .'

'Take them,' said Tessa grandly.

'Oh, thank you!' said the man. 'Let me give you a donation to Telethon,' and he pushed, not a coin, but a five-dollar note into the Money Monkey. Then he picked up the whole carton of empty tobacco tins and set off down the road, carrying it under his arm.

'How much money have we got so far?' asked Lorelei.

'Fifteen dollars,' said Tessa. Her heart sank. If she sat in the tree all night . . . sat there for another twenty hours, say . . . and Mr Martello *did* pay the sponsorship money, which he had promised (partly because he thought Tessa would not last more than an hour or two up the tree), that would mean thirty-five dollars. The hundred–dollar goal seemed to be getting further and further away. *Always remember that wise old saying: 'When the going gets tough, the tough get going,'* Ellington Fillmore had said somewhere in his book. But Ellington Fillmore had not had to sleep in a tree all night.

As evening fell, Tracey and Jackson came skateboarding back again, and the smell of frying fish and hamburgers filled the air. Hungry people came to the Hamburgerama, and some of them crossed the road to see what was going on, just as Tessa had imagined they would.

'She's going to sleep up there all night,' Tracey said over and over again, 'and we're her bodyguards. Pull that rope tighter, Jackson.'

They were busily putting their pup tent up under the tree. It was a small brown tent with a lumberjack painted on one side.

A cheerful, round-faced woman stared hard at Tessa.

'She can't really sleep there,' she said, sounding dismayed.

'She'll have a sleeping bag,' said Pete.

'Good luck, dear,' said a man with sticking-out ears. 'Better you than me!'

Tessa leaned down out of the tree.

'If you think I won't be able to stay here, then sponsor me,' she suggested. 'It won't cost you much, and it's for a good cause.'

'It's not an official event, is it?' asked the first woman.

'It's still on behalf of Telethon,' said Tracey.

'Well, anyone could *say* that,' said the man with sticking–out ears, walking off in the direction of the Hamburgerama.

'Hey, we could have a barbecue here, and then people wouldn't have to go Hamburgerama-ering,' Tracey suggested.

'A barbecue!' exclaimed a deeper voice. It was Tessa's father, Findlay, suddenly appearing in the small crowd. 'Tracey, don't tell me your parents have given you permission to camp out all night on a street corner?' he exclaimed.

'They have, Uncle Findlay. We asked Mum,' cried Jackson quickly.

'I'll bet you rushed in while she was changing the baby and said you were coming round to our place to camp out with Tessa,' said Findlay. Other members of the Fortune family were used to Tracey's cunning ways.

'Well, sort of,' Tracey admitted. 'But Mum is really grateful when we go out. Our house is too small for six kids.'

A familiar truck turned off Main Road and into Bright Street.

'Oh, *oh*!' murmured Pete. This time it was *his* father, Toby, coming to collect him.

'Trace, your mum and dad won't want you

sleeping out on a street corner. And I'm not going to let Tessa sleep up in a tree, so you can just forget all this.'

'Dad!' wailed Tessa. 'I have to. I'm being sponsored. People have paid money. I have to stay up here for twenty-four hours . . . for twenty-one hours now.'

'She's decorated the tree,' said Pete.

Tessa gave him a cross look. This was not a decorated tree. This was a tree with an office in it. Some of the crowd listened with interest. One of them took the sponsorship book from Pete and wrote in an offer, no doubt thinking that Tessa's time in the tree was going to be very short indeed.

'Dad, this is my branch office,' Tessa said. An idea occurred to her. 'It's a high-rise branch office.'

Her father patted the stepladder.

'I suppose this is the ladder of success,' he said, and the passers-by laughed. 'You can stay up there a little longer, but you can't sleep there. That's that.'

'Can she stay up there until midnight?' asked Jackson. 'Then she can sneak down, go to bed, and get back into the tree early in the morning. No-one will know.'

'I've promised not to,' said Tessa.

'Yes, you *creep*, Jackson,' said Tracey. 'A Fortune always keeps a promise.'

'*You* don't,' said Jackson. 'You promised me you'd give me that silver frisbee when I turned nine, and then you didn't.'

Tracey sighed deeply, and shook her head as if Jackson had said something too silly to be worth any sort of explanation.

Uncle Toby had left his truck parked outside Tessa's house.

'What's happening?' he called, as he cantered towards them.

'Tessa wants to sleep in a tree,' said Findlay, 'and I'm telling her she can't.'

At that very moment the sound of music filled the air.

A white van came sailing down Main Road with its windows down and its radio playing loudly. It passed the Bright Street intersection, then slowed down and drew in beside Chillings Superette. But, once the driver had made sure that the street was clear behind him, it backed into Bright Street, parked, and stopped.

TELETHON, Tessa read in giant letters along its side. It made her feel as good as one of Ellington Fillmore's sayings.

A man and a woman got out of the van, and most people under the tree recognized the man at once. His name was Harry Driver, and each night of the week he read the news on television. Just in time, thought Tessa, like the hero in a story.

CHAPTER NINE

'Did I see the word Telethon?' asked Harry Driver as he came up to the tree. 'What's going on here?'

'It's a tree-athon!' cried Jackson, Tracey, Lorelei and Pete, almost together. 'She's staying up there all night.'

Harry Driver read the poster. Then he walked right up to the tree and peered curiously at Tessa.

'Is this your idea?' he asked her.

'I am a branch vice-president, and I've set up my office in the tree,' she declared quickly. 'It's a high-rise branch office. I climbed the ladder of success. People are sponsoring me for Telethon.'

Jackson shook the Money Monkey wildly, doing one of his strange dances.

'She's really Tessa Fortune,' said Tracey. 'Jackson and I are her bodyguards.'

Two other men had scrambled out of the van and were walking towards them. One of them was actually carrying a television camera.

'What do you think, Jock?' asked the first man. 'General human-interest stuff — straight off the street? They might use it.'

'There's not enough light,' one of the newcomers said.

'We got lights in the van. We could run a lead into the hair salon back there,' the other one replied.

'Do you want to be on television, kids?' asked the man who had come up to the tree first. 'Of course you do. Everyone wants to be on the telly. I'm Harry Driver, slaving away out here on the fringes of civilization for the National Telethon. This lovely lady is Stephanie, floor manager and chauffeur. You kids are all in on this together, are you? All your own idea, is it?'

As he talked, Tessa could see one of his helpers going down Main Road to the Top Storey Hair Salon, dragging a length of black flex behind him like a tail. The woman and the third man were unloading lights from the back of the van.

'We started off having a roadside stall,' said

Tracey as if she had been in charge from the very
beginning. Findlay and Toby had stepped back,
and stood silently watching.

'It was all Tessa's idea,' said Pete.

People at the doors of the Hamburgerama
paused to stare over at the tree-athon. Some of
them even stopped playing on the video machine
inside and came out on to the footpath. Tessa
could see that they thought anything worth the
attention of television must be worth their
attention, too.

'We are supporting Telethon,' Tessa cried. 'We want to help old people and raise some money.' *Seize the moment,* Ellington Fillmore had said. Tessa seized it. She began reciting the speech she had planned to give later as she delivered one hundred dollars into grateful hands at the Fairfield Telethon centre. She found she knew it by heart.

Suddenly she was bathed in light from below.

'Everyone should support Telethon because we've all got grandparents, and anyhow, we're all going to be senior citizens ourselves one day,' she ended.

'Great!' said Harry Driver. 'Can you say that all over again in just a moment?'

'She can say it better next time,' said Tracey, smiling proudly at Tessa.

'Silly question!' said Harry Driver, hitting himself lightly on the forehead. 'Of course she can.'

'I'll cue you in, Harry,' said the young woman. 'Don't you watch me, dear. This is just for Harry!'

Harry Driver began talking as if there were someone he had to impress only a metre or so in front of him. His expression suddenly became serious, yet kindly. His voice deepened slightly.

'Telethon action isn't confined to the big cities and the big names,' said Harry Driver. 'Here's a local heroine, Tessa Fortune, conducting her own tree-athon. What's a tree-athon? Well, Tessa is preparing to sleep in a tree all night simply to raise money to help the old folks of the community. Tessa, can you tell us how you came to take on this amazing challenge?'

Tessa ran through her speech again. Tracey was right. This time it sounded even more fluent and sincere than it had the first time round.

'Great work,' said Harry Driver. 'Who says the young people don't care?'

He turned suddenly to Toby and Findlay who were listening in amazement.

'You're part of Tessa's support team, are you?'

Toby and Findlay looked at each other. Findlay sighed.

'You bet we are,' Toby said. 'It's a long time since we were boy scouts, but we haven't forgotten how to camp out, have we, Fin?'

By now a crowd had flocked over from the Hamburgerama, and people were staring up into the tree. Some of them couldn't wait to get stuck into their hamburgers or fish and chips, and began eating them right there, staring at Tessa as if she were already on television. Others watched Stephanie and the rest of the crew pack their equipment and themselves back into the van. Many of these new clients dropped their change into the Money Monkey. One man actually gave ten dollars.

'Will I be on television?' Tessa asked Harry Driver as he helped wind up the last cables.

'Don't know!' he said. 'There's a lot going on. Don't worry! We'll do our best to make a star of you.'

'Shall we use my tent or yours?' Toby asked

Findlay. 'It looks like we'll both be camping out tonight.'

'You're mad, aren't you?' said Findlay. 'But why not? After all, it's for a good cause, isn't it?'

CHAPTER TEN

By the time evening came, there were two tents on the grass under the gum tree. Tracey, Jackson, Lorelei and Pete sat outside one of them. Findlay and Toby had put the other one up for themselves.

Tessa was far more comfortable than she had ever expected to be. Her father and Toby had hoisted an old narrow mattress between the brown fingers of the tree. Though it rather spoiled the look of the office, it would certainly provide a restful surface to sleep on.

'That's great!' Tessa had cried, perched above them, watching Findlay struggling to make it secure. 'I won't be able to stretch myself out, though.'

'You should have thought of that before you started all this,' said Toby. 'Move further up. I need room.'

He was climbing the ladder, pulling up something that looked like a blue fishing net after him. Tessa swarmed to the top of the tallest branch and looked out through the leaves at roof level.

Fish 'n' Cheeps was dark now, but light still spilled from Chillings Superette. Grant stood on the Fish 'n' Cheeps corner watching the tree-athon. He looked small and ghostly now, shrunk by the evening light, and Tessa found herself wondering what it would be like to live in the back of a shop with parents who worked seven days a week from morning to night. Grant had a wonderful bicycle, but no cousins. His father would never put a mattress in a tree for him if ever he needed one.

'There! Try that!' called Findlay, climbing back down the ladder.

Tessa scrambled through a web of ropes. It was a blue, nylon hammock which her father and Toby had found somewhere. It swung between two main branches. Guy ropes led off in all directions. Tessa felt like an executive spider.

'Get into it carefully,' her father warned her.

'You've got to be tactful with hammocks.'

At first it did feel dangerous, as if the hammock might dissolve or turn over sideways. Tessa lay extremely still, staring up into the leaves.

'If you fall out . . .' began Findlay.

Think positively, Ellington Fillmore would say.

'I know I won't fall,' she said quickly.

'*If* you fall, the mattress will be under you,' said Toby. 'After that, it's anyone's guess. But you won't fall,' he added quickly. 'That hammock has been put up by experts.'

'We've all had lots of tree practice,' said Tracey. 'We have secret meetings in the tree behind the grandys' house.'

'How's it going?' asked someone else. A chorus

of voices answered, some of them Fortune voices and some of them the voices of curious clients, keen to give donations to the tree–athon, who consequently felt entitled to join in.

It was Lorelei's parents, Aunt Lorna and Uncle Ivor, walking arm in arm. They had driven over from the smart side of Fairfield to say good night to Lorelei who was squeezing into the small tent with Pete, Tracey and Jackson.

Although he was not one of the Fortune brothers, Tessa enjoyed Uncle Ivor's company because he did not make fun of her when she talked about investments. Nor did he tell her that money wasn't the most important thing in life. He climbed the stepladder and looked into the branch office.

'See my adding machine?' Tessa asked, pointing proudly to her shelf. 'And my desk calendar?'

'I haven't seen an adding machine like that for years,' said Ivor.

'We're going to make a hundred dollars,' Tessa said. 'So far we've got nearly fifty dollars . . . that's counting the twenty dollars that Mr Martello will give me if I stay up here all night. He's sponsoring me at a dollar an hour, and I've been up here four and a half hours already.'

'Telethon's showing on television right now,' said someone down below. 'Tessa won't get a chance to see herself.'

It was only then that Tessa understood she was going to miss seeing almost all the television part of Telethon. She would be up here in the tree until some time tomorrow. She was probably going to miss her own speech.

'Don't worry,' Findlay said. 'We'll load up the video. And remember, you can always change your mind and come down.'

'No,' Tessa said. She had set her goals. She was determined. All the same, suddenly there was something chilly about the shop lights and streetlights, and the night beyond them.

Then Findlay and Toby left to have proper cooked dinners, saying they would be back later. Tessa's house was only a few metres away, but it felt spooky watching the grown-ups walk off.

Ivor opened the door of his Jaguar, parked behind Toby's truck. He climbed halfway into it, and then he hesitated. At last he came back to the tree, carrying something as if it were precious.

'You can borrow this,' he said, handing that something up to Tessa. 'Keep in touch!'

It was his cellular phone. Tessa stared at it as if she couldn't believe her luck.

'You can dial any phone in town,' he said, 'but you have to dial zero-two-eight first to get into the right network. Can you remember that?'

Tessa did not know what to say. The figures 028 blazed in her head. Just for a moment she couldn't help imagining herself punching in a number for New York. 'Sell my shares and buy another lot,' she would say to someone on the other end. 'And put the profits into diamonds.' But she had no reason to make long-distance calls, and no shares, either.

'Thank you, thank you!' she called.

'Look after it,' said Uncle Ivor. 'And remember, it costs sixty cents a minute to make a call on a cellular phone.'

The New York vision went out like a light.

Tracey, who had gone with Jackson to buy fish and chips, came back across the road.

'Maxie gave us the chips free,' she said. 'If we're on television again, we've got to mention his shop.'

Outside Chillings Superette, Grant lingered, looking more and more pathetic, like someone on a desert island watching a party on a faraway beach.

'Shall we let Grant have a few chips?' Pete suddenly suggested.

'Never!' cried Tracey. But Tessa felt full of kindness to Grant. If it hadn't been for him she would not be here up in the tree with Uncle Ivor's cellular phone. She remembered his mother saying, *All he wanted to do was to join in the fun*.

'Ask him over,' she said. 'Tell him we forgive him.'

'You're really weird, Tessa,' said Tracey, but for once she did as she was told.

'Hey, Grant! How about some chips?' she called. 'Come on over. I won't bite your ear off. I've got my own fish and chips now.'

But Grant darted back into the shop as if her kind words were a sort of threat.

More likely clients came by and peered up at

Tessa. Many laughed. A few frowned. As they approached, Jackson leapt up, dancing and holding out the Money Monkey. When they had

walked past, Jackson would tell Tessa how much money he thought they had given. Then Tessa would enter the new sum on the old adding machine, pull the handle and call out the new total to her cousins, who already knew what it must be. The adding machine simply made it official.

The evening gradually grew quiet. Cars going down Main Road sped past the Hamburgerama and Chillings Superette without stopping. At the foot of the tree, Tracey, Jackson, Pete and Lorelei laughed and talked softly. Every now and then one of them shouted something up to Tessa. After a while she began to feel cut off, even lonely, particularly when they began to take it in turns to go into Tessa's house to watch the Telethon on television.

'Have I been on yet?' she asked each returning cousin, but the answer every time was 'no'.

Always remember, it is lonely at the top, Ellington Fillmore had said.

'I'm at the top,' Tessa muttered to herself.

All over town images of television newsreaders in funny hats, laughing and saying what great, *generous* people New Zealanders were, would be flickering in most houses. And here she was, up a tree, with hours and hours and hours and hours to go before she could come down to earth again. For the first time in her life, being up in a tree seemed a terrible ordeal. Tessa turned on the torch and looked at the cellular phone. She tapped in 028 and then her own phone number. Her sister, Prue, answered the phone.

'Prue, this is Tessa, up a gum tree,' she said.

'How's it going?' asked Prue in a comfortable voice.

'Have I been on television yet?'

'Not yet . . . we're all waiting for it, though.'

'What's the national total?'

'I don't know! About eighty thousand dollars, I think. But it's only just begun, and you know how they save the really huge amounts till the very last.'

Tessa reckoned she had talked about sixty cents worth of cellular phone-time.

'I'm getting into my sleeping bag now,' she said. 'Good-night!'

She wormed her way into the sleeping bag, then very carefully rolled herself into the hammock, which swayed and sagged alarmingly. Her bottom was only about three centimetres above the mattress. As she settled down, the strangeness of the night, of being suspended in a tree, feeling like a spider in the middle of a web, swept over her. She clasped the phone to her heart.

A solitary possible client went by. Jackson leaped out, rattling the Money Monkey, and the man dropped in a coin. The lights went out first in Chillings Superette and then in the Hamburgerama. Tessa heard the Chilling car take off somewhere, sounding loud and irritable. Sixteen hours to go. *Sixteen!* She wasn't even halfway through her tree-athon.

'I'll never go to sleep,' Tessa thought. 'I'll be awake all night.' But she did go to sleep soon after. She hung in her hammock like a butterfly in its chrysalis, and did not hear her father and Toby scramble into their tent, half-grumbling, half-laughing as they did so. She floated in and out of sleep, swinging in the hammock up in the tree, the phone held over her heart. Sometimes her eyes opened and she looked up through the leaves and saw a star or two overhead. But she did not wake properly again until a milk truck went rattling by in the grey light of early morning, and the last day of the Telethon began.

CHAPTER ELEVEN

At three o'clock the following afternoon, when Tessa finally came down from the tree, she felt she was setting foot on an undiscovered planet. The Fortune family, including her grandparents, were there to welcome her, just as if she had been away for years, and not simply in her own high-rise branch office for twenty hours. Mr Martello was also there with a small crowd of neighbours and onlookers.

'Congratulations!' he said, and gave her a twenty-dollar note. 'I didn't expect to be paying out this much, I can tell you.'

'That makes eighty-three dollars and thirteen cents,' said Pete, taking the money from her and pushing it into the Money Monkey.

'You owe me an extra fifty cents,' Tessa said. 'I was up there for twenty and a half hours. I'd have stayed there longer but I have to go to the studio now.'

'You Fortunes are a tough bunch,' said Mr Martello as he gave her an extra fifty cents. Tessa handed it to Pete.

'Eighty-three dollars and sixty-three cents,' Pete cried.

'Have I been on television yet?' asked Tessa.

She had asked that question regularly all morning as relatives came and went, but her interview with Harry Driver had not been shown.

Even though she had done what she had set out to do, Tessa had a curious, floating feeling that was very like disappointment. She had not made a hundred dollars, yet she couldn't bear to sit in the tree another moment.

'We'll all chip in to bring the total up,' said Uncle Peter, Tracey's father.

'It's wonderful to have you back on earth again,' said her mother, and hugged her. A sound of clapping reached Tessa's ears. Across Main Road, Mr Sampson of the Hamburgerama was applauding her. On the other side of Bright Street, Grant Chilling and Conrad Eddy watched in silence.

'Let's take the money in now,' said Tessa. 'I want to get rid of it.'

The Good Fortunes Gang crowded into the back of Toby's truck, drove to the Fairfield Town Hall, and joined the queue of people waiting to pass in Telethon contributions.

Everyone in the queue was friendly. People gossiped and compared notes. A woman in front of them had held a knit-athon. She had knitted cardigans for babies and had raised two hundred and seventy-five dollars. A little girl of five had been sponsored to tidy her room and had earned four dollars.

Inside the hall, a scattered audience was watching a local band play rather wearily. By evening the hall would be crowded again, and everyone would be watching the national total flash up on the big screen behind the stage, and waiting to sing the Telethon theme song. Tessa had imagined herself being part of this crowd, but all she wanted now was to be at home, watching the television from her usual chair, with her father and mother and sister, Prue.

'And here's another contributor,' cried one of the hostesses, swooping on Tessa. There were no television cameras. Indeed, there was almost no-one watching this great moment.

'Is Harry Driver here?' Tessa asked.

'He's taking a coffee break, love!' said the hostess. 'They've been on the go all night, and he's heading back to the city in a few minutes.'

Tessa passed the Money Monkey over and tried to remember the speech she had made so well yesterday, but not a word of it came back to her.

'This money is from the Good Fortunes Gang,' she said at last. 'It's a hundred dollars.'

'Wonderful!' cried the hostess. 'That's amazing. A hundred dollars. And you earned it all yourselves?'

'We made eighty-three dollars, sixty-three

cents ourselves,' Tessa said truthfully.

'Wonderful. Thank you all *so* much,' said the hostess, and Tessa saw her eyes were already moving on to the next person in the queue.

As the Fortune family gang left the Town Hall and walked back to where the truck was waiting for them, someone suddenly called out, 'Hello there, Jungle Queen!' It was Harry Driver himself, making for his van in the car-park.

'She stayed in the tree for twenty-four hours,' cried Jackson, exaggerating only a little. 'She did it, and we've just taken the money in.'

'Eighty-three dollars, sixty-three cents,' said Tracey, 'only our fathers had to add some to make it up to a hundred dollars.'

'Great!' cried Harry Driver enthusiastically.

'I wanted to do it myself,' said Tessa. 'I wanted to be the one who raised a hundred dollars with my ideas. And I wanted to be on television.'

'Look, I tried,' said Harry. 'But you're competing with Miss New Zealand, the Prime Minister, rock stars . . . all the heavies! Just relax and go with the flow, kid. And have fun! That's partly what it's all about you know. Fun!' Then he was gone.

Later that night, bathed and clean, Tessa sat between her parents, with Prue and the Fortune

cousins around her, watching the last half-hour of
the Telethon on the television screen. The
Telethon wandering cameraman was out in the
street where Cliff Harding, the front man for the
evening news, was standing on the back of a
lorry, auctioning various things which people had
donated to raise money for this good cause.

'And then there's this!' he cried. 'One of our
vans brought it in from the Fairfield-Rangatiki
area where they're all so artistic. How's this for a
memento of the Telethon!'

Tessa stared. Suddenly there it was: *her* picture of the dancing senior citizens and the white elephant! Someone, perhaps Harry Driver himself, had picked it up in the streets of Fairfield. Someone had liked it and carried it all the way to the city and propped it up among the auction goods, just for fun. There was no doubt about it. It *was* her picture. The camera focused on it. Tessa could remember drawing every line of it. Yet there on the screen in front of her, it looked better than she remembered it, and as remote as if it had been drawn by someone else. Her picture looked like art.

Someone bid two dollars for it. And then a man in a trendy suit bid twenty. Tessa's mouth fell open. So did her mother's.

'That's a generous bid,' said Cliff Harding. 'You must think it's a good cause, sir.'

'I just like the picture,' said the man. Cliff Harding went on to auction something else, but, as her family shouted and exclaimed around her, Tessa watched what was going on in the background. The man in the trendy suit paid the money and claimed her picture . . . his picture now . . . and then walked away with it. He moved out of focus. His figure blurred and vanished, and her picture vanished with him.

'You did make a hundred dollars, after all,' said Tracey, looking at Tessa with a sort of puzzled respect.

'How *did* it happen?' cried Jackson. 'It's like magic.'

'Amazing things do happen,' said Tessa's father. 'Last night I was talking to a bloke I know — Jack Fern, who runs an antique shop over in Rotorua — and apparently he had a real stroke of luck . . . picked up a lot of old tobacco tins dirt cheap.'

'Who'd want old tobacco tins?' asked Tracey.

'People collect them. And these were good ones,' said Uncle Peter. 'Fifteen old tobacco tins in mint condition . . . not dented, not rusty. He reckons he'll get twelve dollars apiece for them. That's a hundred and eight dollars picked up off the side of the road. Now, how's that for good luck?'

'Yaaaaah!' cried a voice in Tessa's head. It was just as if the ghost of Grant Chilling on a ghostly bicycle were riding through her thoughts. The world around her shivered.

But she took a deep breath and smiled. Suddenly she felt she understood something she had not understood before. Even with a whole bookful of good advice from Ellington Fillmore, the world of an executive vice-president was just like a fairy-tale after all. Sometimes you had good luck, and sometimes you had bad luck. Tessa flopped back in her chair, and right then, she began to think about the possibility of being a famous artist instead of an executive vice-president. After all, she had already sold a picture, even if it was by accident, and if she had taken the first step on the ladder of success, shouldn't she keep going until she got to the top?

THE END